The Last Dinosaur

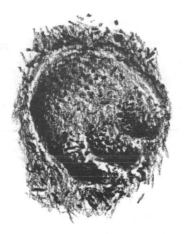

Andrew Whitmore

sundance

a black dog book

Published by Sundance Publishing
P.O. Box 1326, 234 Taylor Street, Littleton, MA 01460
800-343-8204

Copyright © text Andrew Whitmore

First published 1999 as Phenomena by
Horwitz Martin
A Division of Horwitz Publications Pty Ltd
55 Chandos St., St. Leonards NSW 2065 Australia

Exclusive United States Distribution: Sundance Publishing

ISBN 0-7608-8038-7

Printed in Canada

Contents

Author's Note

I've never been to Africa, and I've certainly never hunted dinosaurs. But that's the great thing about being a writer. You can go anywhere and do anything you like—in your imagination.

So do I really believe dinosaurs still live in a remote part of central Africa today? Like trying to find Big Foot, no one really knows the answer.

Eyewitness reports certainly sound convincing. But then you start thinking about the lack of hard evidence to back them up. Why have no bones or other remains ever been discovered, for example?

If these great beasts really have been inhabiting the area for more than 65 million years, surely they must have left some trace behind.

The case is still open as far as I'm concerned. There are plenty of dreamers, a lot braver and more adventurous than I, who will never give up trying to find these beasts.

Andrew Whitmore has been writing ever since he could hold a pen. Science fiction and fantasy stories are his favorites. He has written two novels and loves to read.

5

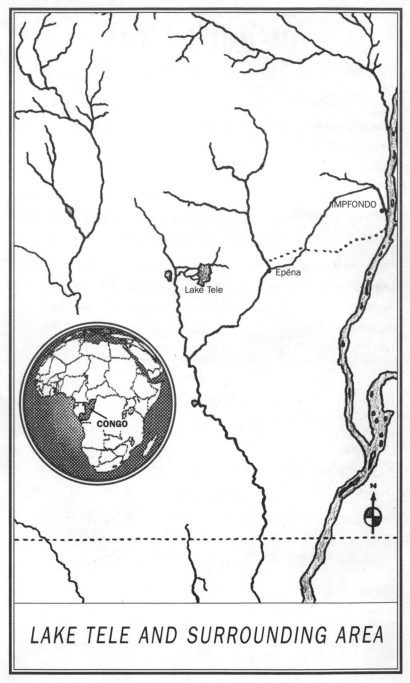

IMPFONDO

Epéna

Lake Tele

CONGO

LAKE TELE AND SURROUNDING AREA

Chapter 1

My Dad, the Dino Hunter

<u>Fact</u>: Africa is the world's second largest continent. It's about one and a half times larger than the United States and Canada put together.

OTHER KIDS' fathers have normal jobs. They are firefighters, plumbers, accountants, lion tamers. But not my dad. Oh, no.

Every year it's the same. Career Week comes around, and I have to get up and make a complete fool of myself.

"All right, Gina," Ms. Simonson said. "Go ahead."

I tried explaining that no one would really be interested in what my father did. But Ms. Simonson is hard to budge once she makes up her mind.

"Nonsense, Gina," she said. "I'm sure the class will enjoy hearing your presentation."

And so they would. One or two of them were giggling already. Best to just get it over with, I thought.

I took a deep breath and began.

"Ms. Simonson, my father is a—"

"Fruitcake!" someone called out.

It was Brad Jenkins, of course. He always gave me a hard time about my dad. In fact, fruitcake was a lot more polite than most of the words he used.

I felt the blood rushing to my cheeks. Just about everyone was laughing now. "He is not!" I snapped. "He's a scientist!"

"That's enough," Ms. Simonson said, glaring at the class until they quieted down. "Thank you. Now, let's start again, shall we? Without any interruptions this time." She looked across at me. "I believe you were telling us that your father is a scientist?"

I nodded. "That's right."

"How interesting," Ms. Simonson said. "And what exactly does he study?"

"Animals," I said carefully, hoping she'd be satisfied with that.

"So he's a zoologist then?"

"Sort of," I said.

Ms. Simonson raised her eyebrows.

"What do you mean 'sort of,' Gina?"

"Well, he—I mean—" I tried to think of some way of putting it that didn't sound really dumb. "He's a cryptozoologist," I said. At least that had an impressive ring to it. But I knew Ms. Simonson wasn't going to let me off that easily.

"Cryptozoologist?" she said, sounding rather puzzled. "That's a new one on me, Gina. Can you explain what your father actually does?"

I thought about just making something up. But Brad Jenkins had already raised his hand. No doubt he would be only too happy to tell Ms. Simonson if I didn't.

"He studies unknown animals," I said miserably.

"I'm not sure I understand," Ms. Simonson said.

"You know," Brad said. "Like the Loch Ness Monster and that." He put on a silly face. "Better get your father, Gina. I think I'm turning into Big Foot."

Ms. Simonson didn't even bother telling him off this time. "I see," she said. "Well, that's very . . . interesting. Thank you, Gina. You can sit down now."

cryptozoologist: Someone who searches for previously undiscovered animals.

I hurried back to my desk. I tried hard not to look at anyone. But I couldn't help hearing Brad mutter, "Fruitcake!" as I walked past.

Ms. Simonson picked up her chalk. "I'm not sure where Gina's father's occupation should go," she said, looking at the lists up on the board. "Let's just put it under OTHER, shall we? Gina, you might have to spell that one for me, I'm afraid."

"C-R-Y-P-T-O," I said miserably, as the rest of the class copied it down. "Z-O-O-L-O-G-I-S-T."

In my own project book, however, I just wrote FRUITCAKE.

After all, they meant pretty much the same thing.

Dad was waiting at the gate when I arrived home. He had an envelope in one hand and a broad smile on his face.

"I got some fantastic news, sweetheart," he said, waving the envelope in front of me. "Guess who this is from."

I wasn't really in the mood for games, especially after what happened at school.

But Dad didn't seem to notice. He was obviously excited about something.

"Just the ICS!" he announced proudly. "That's who!"

"ICS?" I said absently. I hadn't the slightest idea what he was talking about.

"You know," he said. "The International Cryptozoological Society. I wrote to them months ago. I was looking for someone to sponsor the Mokele-Mbembe project."

That rang a bell. "Oh, yeah," I said. "You were telling me about it last semester. How there's supposed to be a dinosaur or whatever living in—"

Suddenly, it all clicked. I threw down my bag, staring at Dad in disbelief.

"Africa?"

Dad was grinning. "Uh-huh."

"Africa!"

Next thing I knew I was whirling through the air as Dad spun me around in his arms. "AFRICA!" I squealed. "AFRICA!" I couldn't wait to tell the kids at school. They'd be green with envy.

Mokele-Mbembe (*mo-kay-lee mmm-bem-be*): A large, unidentified animal believed to be living in the rain forest of central Africa.

"So when do we go?" I asked.

Dad finally put me down. "What's that?" he said.

"When do we go?" I repeated. "I mean, is it soon? I'll have to tell Ms. Simonson so she can give me some work to take with me. We'll need to get some gear too, I guess. And aren't you supposed to take malaria tablets or something?"

I noticed Dad was looking at me strangely. I began to feel a knot in my stomach.

"I am going, aren't I, Dad?"

"Well," he began. "You see—"

"But we're a team, remember!" We'd been just about everywhere together. Along the Himalayas hunting the Abominable Snowman. Around Loch Ness to check for the monster. We even went searching for Big Foot. Mom had come too—before she and Dad split up. We had a fantastic time. Camping out in the woods. Cooking over an open fire. Sleeping under the stars . . .

> malaria: A tropical disease spread by a mosquito after biting an infected person.

"I'm sorry, Gina," Dad said. "It's just too dangerous."

"You're going," I pointed out.

"Yeah, but I'm a

grown-up. Central Africa is really no place for kids."

"But it's not fair! I could handle it."

Dad put his arm around me again. He looked sad. "Don't worry," he said. "We'll be able to keep in touch. I'm going to post daily reports on the Net. I'll even have a digital camera with me, so there'll be pictures as well. And we can email each other anytime we like."

"That's not the same as actually being there," I said.

"I guess not." Dad picked up my bag and hefted it over his shoulder. "Come on," he said. "I'll show you where I'm off to on the map."

"All right," I said as we headed up the driveway. "It still isn't fair though."

"I know it isn't, sweetheart," Dad said. "But I won't be gone for long. And when I get back, you'll be able to tell everyone that your dad was the man who discovered the world's last living dinosaur. I'll even let you name it if you like. How about that?"

"Really?" I asked.

13

"Sure. There are certain rules, of course, but you would make the final choice."

"Wow!" I said.

That would certainly wipe the smirk off Brad Jenkins's face!

Mom came to pick me up on Sunday night.

Dad and I spent all weekend planning how to break the news. But we didn't really come up with anything. In the end, I just blurted it out as soon as Mom walked in the door.

Her reaction was pretty much what we expected.

"Are you totally out of your mind?" she said.

Dad looked at her sheepishly. "There won't be any problems," he said. "The ICS personnel are arranging everything. It'll all go like clockwork."

"Have you any idea what things are like in central Africa at the moment?"

"There's a bit of trouble, but—"

"A bit!" Mom rolled her eyes. "For heaven's sake, Raf, don't you watch the news? It's crazy down there right now."

"I'll be all right," Dad told her.

"That's all you ever say, isn't it? I'll be all right. Don't you think it's about time you started acting a little more responsibly? I mean—"

"Excuse me," I interrupted. "But if you're going to fight, I think I'll go outside for a while."

"It's okay, sweetheart," Dad said. "No one's fighting. We're just having a discussion, that's all."

"In other words," Mom said, "I'm trying to talk some sense into your father. I don't know why I bother. I mean, he's come up with some pretty crazy schemes in the past. But this one really takes the cake."

I sighed. Mom and Dad hardly ever agree on anything. Mom's a doctor, and she's really glamorous. (At least I think so, anyway.) She wears nice clothes and trendy glasses. Her curly black hair always looks really stylish. As for Dad—well, he's just about the exact opposite. He hardly ever combs his hair and wears the same old clothes most of the time.

Mom says he's the smartest man she's ever met. He could be a professor at some university if he wanted to, making lots of money. Instead, he just does a bit of casual work at the local college. The

schemes: *Plans or programs of action.*	
trendy: *The current style or fashion.*	

rest of the time he's off on what Mom calls his wild-goose chases. I guess she thought going all the way to Africa on one was just the last straw.

Dad, of course, saw things differently.

"This is the big time, Mary," he said. "I've dreamed about this all my life."

"Dreams don't pay the bills, Raf," Mom said. "And they aren't going to help put Gina through school."

Now they were arguing. Things always got ugly when they talked about money.

I tugged at Mom's sleeve. "We'd better get going," I said. "You were going to help me with my math homework tonight, remember?"

"All right," Mom said. "I suppose I'm just wasting my breath anyway."

Dad gave me a sly wink as he handed over my bag. "See you later, sweetheart."

"Bye, Dad," I said, kissing him on the cheek. "I'll see if the library has anything on that place you told me about. What was its name again?"

"Congo."

Mom shook her head in disgust. "Better you than me," she said.

I spent the next four weekends helping Dad prepare for his expedition.

The guidebooks I borrowed from the library weren't much help. Most didn't even mention Congo. Those that did listed many reasons why people shouldn't go there.

I showed them to Dad, but he just shrugged. "Don't worry," he told me. "It's not as if I'll be wandering around on my own. The ICS is arranging for some local guides, including Pygmies, to look after me. They'll keep me out of trouble."

I was still worried, though. Dad didn't even know exactly where he was going. All of the maps he showed me had a lot of blank spaces on them.

"The area has never been surveyed," Dad explained. "Once you head west from the main river, there's nothing but swamp. No one has ever set foot on most of it—except for the Pygmies."

Pygmies: Approximately 250,000 people who live mainly in the rain forests of Africa and Asia and average less than five feet in height. Pygmies are separated into groups by culture and language.

I had read about Pygmies. They sounded amazing. Even I would be taller than most of them. And yet somehow they manage to survive in one of the most dangerous and inhospitable places on earth. Dad said they knew everything there was to know about the rain forest—including where to look for Mokele-Mbembe. He was relying on them to point him in the right direction. Otherwise he could wander through the swamps for years and never find a thing.

Assuming, of course, there was anything to be found in the first place.

"How come no one has ever seen this Mokele-Mbembe?" I asked Dad once. "I mean, something that big would be pretty hard to miss, wouldn't it?"

"That's just the point," Dad said. "Plenty of people have seen it." He handed me a thick file full of photocopies from various books and magazines. "Dozens of sightings have been recorded over the years. Trouble is, they have all been made by locals, so hardly anyone takes them seriously." Dad sounded almost angry. "Exactly the same thing happened when Europeans were first told about gorillas. They just

---

inhospitable: Not a nice place to live, where food and shelter are hard to find.

thought the local people were making it up until one was actually caught."

"So you really think it's out there, Dad?"

"Yes, I do. Otherwise I wouldn't be traveling there to look for it, now would I?"

"No. I guess you wouldn't," I said.

Dad looked at the map, pointing to a lake surrounded by nothing but white space. "That's where he'll be, sweetheart. Lake Tele. And with any luck, I'm going to prove it."

I hoped so, for his sake. None of his previous expeditions had turned up anything spectacular. The odd footprint here and there. A few tufts of what might have been Big Foot hair. Enough to convince Dad he was on the right track. But it wasn't enough to put his name in history books.

I just wished I could be there to share it with him.

The day I'd been dreading finally arrived. Dad had sold his car and just about everything else he owned. So Mom gave him a ride to the airport. I took the day off from school so I could go too. He had already sent most of his gear on ahead, so there was room in the car.

On the way, he showed me the webpage he designed for the expedition. He called it DINOHUNTER. It had only been up and running a few days, but there were already several thousand hits recorded on the counter.

There was a lot of interest in the expedition overseas. Dad even managed to get a few local sponsors to help out. One of the communication companies supplied a state-of-the-art satellite phone. He would be able to keep in contact no matter where he was. Some adventure travel companies helped out as well.

Dad checked in his bags, and we went to eat lunch. He kept joking about the expedition, but I couldn't help feeling sad. I hadn't thought about what it would be like when he was gone. I suddenly realized how much I would miss him.

Dad put off boarding as long as he could, but eventually he was called over the loudspeaker. I remember standing outside the doors to the International Terminal. Tears were streaming down my face. Dad was a bit misty-eyed as well.

"Cheer up," he said. "I'll be back soon."

I gave him a big hug. Mom did too. Dad looked surprised, but I could tell he was pleased.

"Well, I guess this is it," he said. He gave me one

last kiss. "Be a good girl for your mother, okay?"

Then the sliding doors closed behind him. He waved from his seat as the plane moved away from the gate.

Mom and I watched as his plane taxied toward the runway. I waved madly, but I don't think Dad could see me.

The big jumbo jet engines roared louder and louder, and the plane lumbered slowly up into the sky. I kept waving until the plane was nothing more than a tiny speck in the sky.

"He'll be all right, won't he, Mom?" I asked.

She put her arms around me. "Of course he will," she said. "It's not as if he'll be gone forever. We'll have plenty to keep us occupied while he's gone."

At least she was right about one thing.

Chapter 2
Vanished!

DAD CALLED US from Paris to test his new phone.
He was waiting for his connecting flight to
Brazzaville. I told him to take a picture of the Eiffel
Tower for me. He said that would be a bit hard
seeing as how he was stuck at the airport.

It was funny talking by satellite phone. The signal
took a few seconds to travel back and forth, so we
kept cutting each other off. We chatted a while
longer, but then he had to go.

Hearing his voice made me feel sad again, and I
wanted to cry. Mom said I should go to bed, but I
couldn't sleep. I just stared at the ceiling trying to
imagine what Dad was doing.

When I checked the computer the next morning,
there were a few new email messages but nothing

from Dad. His webpage hadn't been updated either. It still showed the picture of him in his shorts and sun hat that he uploaded before he left. He looked more like someone heading off to the beach than an explorer.

Everyone at school knew about the trip. A few articles appeared in the local paper, but they tended to treat the whole thing as a joke. One cartoon showed Dad examining the rain forest through a magnifying glass. A silly-looking dinosaur towered behind him. The caption read, "I could have sworn it was around here somewhere."

Brad Jenkins brought a copy of the cartoon to class and put it up on the bulletin board. Then he added a few touches of his own, giving the dinosaur a fake mustache and sunglasses. "That's why no one can find it," he told the class. "It's in disguise."

Everyone thought he was hilarious. I just ignored him until the end of class.

I went to get a snack before I checked the computer again after school. I was still feeling annoyed with Brad Jenkins when I saw an email from Dad had arrived. The computer seemed to take forever to open up his message.

It was a relief to know he arrived safely. And he
sounded quite cheerful too, despite the heat and his
hassles with the phone. But then I guess he had every
reason to be.

The Great Dino Hunt was on!

———

Once things settled down, I didn't miss Dad so
much. I still thought about him a lot and wondered
what he was doing. But at least I wasn't feeling so

24

upset every time something reminded me of him. I guess I was getting used to him not being around.

We still kept in close contact. He sent at least two emails a day. Together with the photos on his webpage, they kept me up-to-date on what he was doing.

Mom and I went to the movies a few times, and we did something special together on the weekends. If I felt really depressed, Mom let me call Dad on his satellite phone. Hearing his voice always made me feel better.

He was making good progress now. It had taken him a while to sort out everything in Brazzaville. I got the impression that it was a bit of a madhouse there. But he finally managed to get a flight to a place called Impfondo. It was only about 60 miles from Lake Tele. The head of the wildlife group there was a big help. He organized a boat to take Dad down the river. If everything went according to plan, he would reach the lake in a matter of days.

The photos he took of the rain forest were stunning. It looked exactly like the place where you'd expect to find a dinosaur, which isn't surprising. According to Dad, nothing much has changed there for 65 million years.

I was a bit disappointed when I saw the photos of my dad's guides. He told me they were Pygmies, so I was expecting them to look a lot more exotic or something. But they turned out to be just like anybody else. They didn't even look that short. And both of them were certainly better dressed than Dad. Or perhaps it only seemed that way because their clothes weren't constantly soaked in sweat the way his were.

He sent an email just before he set off from Impfondo:

> **Subject: Wish me luck!**
> **Date: Fri. Sept. 29 - 06:37:05 +0100**
> From: <rPatrioni@dinohunt.com>
> To: <gina@worldnet.com>
>
> Dear Gina:
> This is it. I'm off. I'll put a picture of our boat on the webpage. It's called a dugout, which is a boat made from a single huge tree trunk.
> We're going to stop at a few villages along the way to check out reported sightings of Mokele-Mbembe. I can't wait.
>
> I'll keep you posted.
> Love, Dad

And that was the last we heard from him. I wasn't really worried at first. I just assumed he was having problems with his satellite phone. He could hardly just pop into the nearest Internet site and log in from there.

After a few days, however, I started getting nervous. If his phone was broken, he wouldn't be able to let anyone know if he was in trouble. Anything could have happened to him.

I felt sick to my stomach. Dad could be lost for all I knew.

Or dying.

Mom told me not to be so dramatic. She was sure there must be a simple explanation why we hadn't heard from him.

Then the phone call arrived.

I could tell by the look on Mom's face that something was wrong. Her face went as white as a sheet.

I tried to work out what was going on. All Mom said was "Are you sure?" and "I see" and "Of course." She sounded quite calm, but her hand was shaking when she hung up the phone.

"What is it?" I said. "What's happened?"

"That was Jim Thompson," Mom told me. "He runs the wildlife group in Impfondo. He said a health worker in one of the villages along the river found a big dugout washed up on the bank. Apparently he told Jim about it, thinking it belonged to him. Jim thinks it must be your father's boat."

I suddenly felt all cold and empty inside. Some things are so horrible to think about they just leave you numb.

"I'm sure there's nothing to worry about," Mom said. "There must be lots of dugouts on the river. It could have belonged to anyone."

"Then why hasn't Dad been in touch?" I asked. I was starting to tremble now. Then my legs seemed to give out beneath me. Mom caught me in her arms and sat me down in a chair.

"Are you all right?" she asked.

I hardly heard her. My mind was racing. The boat must have capsized or something. But Dad was a good swimmer. He would have made it to the bank okay. I pictured him wandering through the brilliant green rain forest. Lost. Maybe injured as well. There was obviously only one thing to do.

"We have to find him, Mom!" I shouted.

She just looked at me.

"We have to!" I repeated. "We have to!"

"Now, now," Mom said, stroking my hair. "Everything is going to be just fine. Mr. Thompson says he's going to organize a search party right away, just in case. And I'll try to call the embassy as well. I'm sure they'll be able to help."

"But we should be there, Mom!" I protested. "Dad needs us!"

"We'd probably just get in the way," Mom said. I noticed her expression harden a little. "Besides, your father knew the risks he was taking. If anything did go wrong, he's got no one to blame except himself."

I just stared at her. I couldn't believe my ears. I knew Mom and Dad hadn't always gotten along, but I never thought she would turn her back on him. "You hate him, don't you?" I said. "You want him to die."

embassy: *A government's official headquarters in a foreign country.*

Mom looked shocked. "Of course I don't hate him. But I can't be expected to drop everything and go halfway around the world simply because one of his schemes has gone wrong. I've got my patients to think about and . . . where do you think you're going?"

I stormed out of the room without even looking at her, slamming the door behind me. I didn't care about her patients. I didn't care how far away Africa was. I just wanted my dad back.

The next few days were a nightmare. My heart skipped a beat every time the phone rang. I was sure it was someone calling to say they found Dad's body.

Mom and I still weren't speaking. She let me stay home from school—not that she had a choice. I wasn't going anywhere until I knew Dad was all right.

I wasn't sleeping very well. The rain forest kept invading my dreams. I'd wake up shouting Dad's name, my pajamas soaked with sweat. No wonder I felt like a zombie most of the time.

frazzled: Extremely tired or worn out.

Mom looked frazzled, too. If she wasn't answering phone calls, she was making them. Our government representatives weren't much help. The man Mom spoke to said Dad shouldn't have gone there in the first place. She told him it was nice to know the government took so much interest in the welfare of its citizens. Then she banged down the phone. I was surprised it didn't snap in half.

In fact, just about everyone appeared to have written Dad off. The International Cryptozoological Society said they were sorry to hear about his disappearance. But they couldn't afford to send anyone to look for him. The Congo government acted as if he never existed. Even though Mom spoke French quite well, they pretended not to understand what she was talking about. They kept switching her from one department to the next.

Only Jim Thompson seemed to be on our side. He contacted every village along the river. He asked if anyone knew of Dad's whereabouts or of any other members of the expedition. But everywhere he went he drew a blank.

At least we knew it was definitely Dad's boat that was found. Mr. Thompson had checked it out personally. He also searched as much of the surrounding area as he could. But it was like looking for a needle in a haystack. The rain forest was very thick in places. You could pass within a few feet of someone and not even see them.

He told us not to give up hope. As long as Dad had the Pygmies with him, he'd be fine. They knew the rain forest inside and out, and would have no trouble living off the land. After all, they'd been doing it for thousands of years.

But what if Dad was on his own? How long would he survive alone?

Mom didn't ask Mr. Thompson that. Deep down, I think we both knew the answer.

I was tossing and turning so much I couldn't sleep. My throat was dry, so I decided to get a drink of water. When I turned on the kitchen light, I saw Mom sitting at the table with her head in her hands. There were dark circles around her eyes. She seemed to have aged about ten years.

I suddenly realized how tough the past few days must have been on her. My sulking couldn't have made things any easier either.

Feeling pretty ashamed of myself, I shuffled up beside her and put my arms around her shoulders. I gave her a hug.

sulking: Being depressed and silent.

"Are you all right, Mom?" I asked.

She looked up. "I've been better," she said. "What's the matter? Can't sleep?"

I shook my head.

"Me neither." Mom patted the chair next to her. "Here," she said, "sit down a minute. I think there's something we need to talk about."

"I'm sorry about how I've been acting," I told her. "It's just that—you know—with Dad missing and everything . . ."

"Don't worry," Mom said. "I understand how you must feel. But just because your father and I separated doesn't mean I don't care about him."

"I know, Mom," I said.

"I hoped things would have worked themselves out by now, but they obviously haven't. So . . ." Mom took a deep breath, "I've decided to go to Africa after all."

I jumped up from my chair and threw my arms around her. "You mean it?"

"Well, there doesn't seem to be anything more I can do from this end. And it won't be so easy for the Congo government to ignore me if I'm actually camped out on their doorstep."

"All right, Mom!" I cried. I wasn't sure whether I

was laughing or crying—both probably. "I knew you wouldn't let Dad down!"

Mom grinned. "You know me. I'm just a big softie at heart."

I suddenly had a dreadful thought. "You're not planning on leaving me behind, are you?"

"What would be the point?" Mom said. "You'd probably try to swim to Africa or something. No, I don't care what anybody says. We're doing this together. If the two of us can't find your father, no one can."

"And . . ."

"And what?"

"Well . . . he will still be alive, won't he? I mean . . ."

Mom cupped my face in her hands and looked me square in the eye. "He'd better be," she said darkly. "Because I intend to kill him for putting us through all this."

Chapter 3
Into Africa

STEPPING OFF the plane at Brazzaville was like walking into a sauna.

If it got this hot at night, I shuddered to think what the days would be like. A misty rain was falling, turning to steam as it hit the tarmac.

Still, it was a relief to be out in the open. Mom and I had spent the last 22 hours either sitting in planes or hanging around airports. I'd been overseas before to Scotland and Nepal. And another time we went to visit the little village in Italy where Dad's parents came from. But I had forgotten how cramped and noisy planes were.

tarmac: The paved runway a plane uses to take off from and land on.

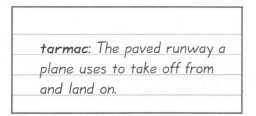

The trip to Paris seemed to take forever. It was like being cooped up in a room for eight hours straight with all the windows closed. Except this room creaked and hummed constantly. I was too uncomfortable to sleep and too tired to read. We couldn't even see the movie screen well from where we were sitting.

Mom had worked miracles to get us here. Once she makes up her mind to do something, nothing stands in her way.

The Congo embassy told us it would take at least two weeks to arrange our visas to Africa. Then our government said they couldn't help. Mom threatened to call every current affairs program in the country. She would explain how the government was leaving her husband for dead in the middle of Africa. Half an hour later they called back. They said the visas would arrive by courier the next day.

Arranging our tickets wasn't easy, either. Mom went to one of the adventure tour companies that had sponsored Dad's expedition. A guy called Steve spent about 20 minutes explaining that it might be difficult traveling in Congo. It was especially tough for women on their own. He thought Mom was out of her mind to even consider taking me along. Mom listened carefully, then said, "I know all that. Now how much are the tickets?"

I guess Steve knew when he was beaten. He gave us

the phone number of someone in Brazzaville. He said this person might be able to help us.

"His name's Marcellin N'dossa," Steve told us. "He's an ex-park ranger who leads some of our tours. I think he comes from Impfondo, so he ought to know his way around."

I asked Steve if that meant Marcellin was a Pygmy, but he just laughed.

"No, no," he said. "He's a Bantu like most Congolese. The Pygmies keep pretty much to themselves. You really only find them in the deep forest."

He booked us on the next available flight. We waited for our visas to arrive, then drove straight to the airport. I didn't even have time to ask Ms. Simonson for some work. As things turned out, I wouldn't have been able to do it anyway.

Mom gave me about a thousand different injections. I didn't know there were that many diseases in the world, let alone in just one country. We also had to take these tiny pills every day to stop us from getting malaria. They tasted horrible.

Bantu: A large group of people living mainly in central and southern Africa.

But at least we weren't half a world

away from Dad anymore. In fact, Impfondo was only about 435 miles from Brazzaville. You could get there in a couple of hours by plane.

At this rate, we'd have Dad back before we knew it.

———————————

The first thing I noticed about Brazzaville was the soldiers. Mom said she thought they looked really handsome in their neat khaki uniforms and red berets. The machine guns they carried made me a little nervous though. I couldn't help wondering exactly who they were planning to use them against.

The city was amazing. Our taxi shared the road with horse-drawn carriages and the occasional flock of goats. There were plenty of modern office blocks. But other buildings looked like something out of

Gone With the Wind, with tall white columns on the front balconies. The streets were crowded with all kinds of people. Some were dressed in brightly colored robes. But just as many wore Western-style business suits or baseball caps and T-shirts. There were street stalls offering

everything from fresh fish to live monkeys and mountains of tropical fruit. I was overwhelmed by the exotic sights, sounds, and smells pouring through the taxi window. It was wonderful.

We went to the same hotel Dad stayed in. He was right about the heat. Our room was stifling. All the big ceiling fans seemed to do was stir up more hot air. At least the shower worked, so Mom and I were able to wash off.

It was a bit cooler out on the patio. We stayed there awhile, sipping ice-cold water and looking out across the Congo River. Its muddy brown waters seemed to stretch forever. Huge mats of purple, blue, and yellow flowers floated lazily along with the current. There were palms everywhere, their leaves as bright and glossy as plastic. Other trees reminded me of the trees back home, smothered in pink blossoms.

"Well," Mom said. "Here we are. It's hard to believe, isn't it?"

"Sure is," I said. "I don't know why everyone tried to talk us out of coming here. Doesn't seem that bad to me."

Mom took a deep breath. Even this far from the river you could smell the flowers. "It's beautiful," she said. "Of course, a little air-conditioning wouldn't hurt."

"So what did this Marcellin guy sound like?" I asked. Mom had called him as soon as we arrived. He was coming to the hotel that afternoon. "Will he help us?"

"I hope so," Mom said. "He was very polite on the phone. But I guess we won't really know until we meet him."

"I guess not," I said.

Mom rattled the ice in her glass. "More water?" she asked.

"Yes, please," I told her. "I'm still very thirsty."

Marcellin was a lot younger than I expected—in his twenties, I guess. His skin was the color of charcoal, and he walked with confidence.

He looked a bit like a Boy Scout leader in his khaki shorts, military-style shirt, and knee-length socks. All he needed was the hat. Of course, none of the Scout leaders I knew wore a holster on their hip. And they weren't as handsome either.

I felt rather shabby in my sarong and T-shirt, but they were the coolest things I brought. I wondered how Marcellin managed to look so neat and trim. It was really hot outside, and he hadn't even raised a sweat.

"Madame Patrioni?" he said.

Mom brushed a strand of hair from her eyes and smiled. "That's right. You must be Mr. N'dossa."

They shook hands.

"This is my daughter, Gina," Mom said.

Marcellin shook my hand as well. "It is a pleasure to meet you, mademoiselle," he said.

He was the first person we met who spoke more than a few words of English. He had a slight French accent. But it was a relief not having to rely on Mom to translate everything.

"Thank you for coming at such short notice," Mom said. "Won't you sit down?"

Marcellin took a seat opposite us and glanced out across the river. "How do

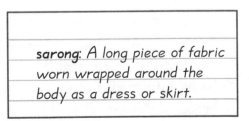

sarong: *A long piece of fabric worn wrapped around the body as a dress or skirt.*

you like our country?" he asked. He looked at me and then at Mom.

"Well, we haven't seen that much of it yet," Mom told him. She turned to me. "But we like it just fine so far, don't we, Gina?"

I nodded enthusiastically. "It's lovely."

"I am glad," Marcellin said. "My friend Stephen tells me you are looking for your husband. That is correct?"

"Yes," Mom told him. "The last we heard he was setting off from Impfondo for the Likouala-aux-Herbes River. Then he just disappeared."

Marcellin looked thoughtful. "I see," he said. "The River of Grasses can be most dangerous. Might I inquire as to the objective of his expedition?"

Mom and I exchanged glances. I think we were both a little embarrassed to admit Dad had been hunting dinosaurs.

"He was investigating reports about an unknown animal that is supposed to live there," she said at last. "I believe the local name for it is Mokele-Mbembe."

"The Stopper of Rivers?" Marcellin flashed a dazzling smile. "Excuse me, madame," he said quickly. "But I am afraid your husband has been badly informed. I can assure you that there is no such beast as Mokele-Mbembe. It is just a story my people tell. Like a fairy tale, you know?"

Mom pursed her lips, and for a moment she said nothing. "Yes, well," she said. "Raf has spent most of his life chasing fairy tales. But that's neither here nor there now. Do you think we stand any chance at all of finding him?"

"Of course we will find him, Madame Patrioni," Marcellin assured her. "All will be well, I promise you."

Marcellin had such an air of confidence about him that all my fears almost disappeared. I grinned from ear to ear. Everything was going to work out fine. I just knew it.

Mom didn't sound convinced. "Let's hope you're right, Mr. N'dossa," she said. "Now, how much do you want for your services?"

Marcellin held up his hand. "Please," he said. "I will be honored to help reunite you with your husband. That is only right and proper. You must not pay me anything."

Mom actually blushed. "That's very kind of you," she murmured.

"It is the least I can do," Marcellin told her. "First, we must see about getting some tickets to Impfondo."

Mom was obviously a lot happier discussing practical matters. She looked relieved. "How soon is the next flight?" she asked.

Marcellin shrugged. "That is hard to say, madame. The plane flies when it can, rather than to any timetable."

I wasn't sure what he meant. But it didn't sound very promising.

"That is one of the things that is not very lovely about Congo, now," Marcellin explained. "But I will do my best. In the meantime, you will need to buy certain items before we leave." He took a pad and pen from one of his shirt pockets. "I will make a list."

We certainly seemed to have hit the jackpot. I couldn't imagine how anything could possibly go wrong now that we had Marcellin to look after us. At this rate, we'd have Dad back safe and sound in no time.

Half of the things on Marcellin's list were snakebite kits.

"How many different kinds of snakes do they have here?" I asked Mom.

"I don't know," she said. "Quite a few I guess."

She glanced at her piece of paper. "Let's see. He says we'll need antivenin for the Gabon viper, the green mamba, the water cobra—"

"All right!" I said. "I get the picture." I had enough fear of snakes. I didn't want to know the details.

The rest of the list included things like lightweight tents, mosquito nets, and chlorine tablets to purify the water. Apparently the swamps around Impfondo were full of parasites. Even boiled water wasn't safe to drink. The rain forest may have looked spectacular, but I was beginning to realize that none of it was particularly friendly.

The hotel manager gave us directions to a shop that stocked what we wanted. Mom and I were both soaked in sweat by the time we got back to the hotel. We took another shower and changed into some fresh clothes. Then it was time to meet Marcellin for dinner.

He had our tickets with him. Apparently a plane for Impfondo would definitely be leaving at six the next morning. We had to make sure we were on it because there was no telling when the next one might be.

Marcellin also arranged the travel

> antivenin: Medicine used to treat people bitten by a poisonous snake.

permits we needed for our trip. Luckily, he had a cousin who worked for the government. He was able to pull a few strings and get them for us right away. Otherwise we could have been stranded in Brazzaville for weeks.

It appeared we were all set to go. Nothing could stop us now.

Marcellin took us to a restaurant near the hotel that served traditional meals. I had roast antelope in some kind of spicy sauce. It was delicious. However, I couldn't help feeling a little guilty about eating something that had been jumping around the rain forest not long ago.

We chatted with Marcellin for a while. He told us what to expect when we got to Impfondo. His stories about growing up in a nearby village were fascinating. They made my own life seem pretty dull. Sometimes during the wet season, gorillas would leave the rain forest in search of food and raid his family's gardens. Leopards were the most dangerous, however. They would crouch in the trees and leap down on unsuspecting children as they wandered past. And I thought I had it tough being chased

> **crouch**: Bend down in a low position with legs held close to the body.

by the neighbors' small dog!

Marcellin walked us back to the hotel after dinner. He said he arranged for another cousin to pick us up at 5:00 a.m. That way we'd be at the airport in plenty of time for our flight. I couldn't see Mom and me having much trouble getting up that early. We hadn't adjusted to the change in time zones yet.

We wished Marcellin a good night and then went up to our room.

"All right," Mom said. "Let's go to bed. We've got an early start tomorrow."

I was far too excited to sleep. I lay awake most of the night, listening to the traffic outside and the drone of insects around my mosquito net. They sounded like a fleet of miniature dive-bombers.

It was hard to believe we'd come so far in such a short space of time. Just two days ago, I was back at home eating my heart out because Dad was lost somewhere in the rain forest. Tomorrow we would be close to where he had disappeared.

"Come on, Dad," I whispered. "Just hang in there a little while longer."

Chapter 4

Rivers of Grass

Fact: The wet season lasts from October to May in central Africa. During this time many roads and rivers cannot be crossed.

IMPFONDO AIRPORT was a tiny strip of asphalt in an ocean of greenery. Looking down at it from the plane, I couldn't believe we were going to land there.

But the pilot knew what he was doing. We touched down without a problem and were soon clambering out onto the tarmac.

The plane was air-conditioned, and I actually dozed off during the trip. Outside, however, it was as hot and muggy as ever. Mom and I were both dripping with sweat long before we reached the small shelter that served as the airport terminal.

Jim Thompson and his wife, Mandy, were waiting for us. They were probably in their mid-fifties and looked amazingly fit and athletic. I suppose you would need to be in a place like this. I wasn't sure what to expect. I had never been in the rain forest before. I couldn't imagine what living here would be like.

We exchanged brief introductions, then Mom got straight down to business.

"Any word about the expedition?" she asked.

Jim shook his head. "Afraid not," he said. "I've been in touch with most of the villages from here to Edzama. But there's been no sign of them yet. We just have to keep our fingers crossed."

"I'm sorry we can't be more helpful," Mandy said. "I know how hard this must be for you and Gina."

"Not at all," Mom said. "You've done more than enough as it is."

Jim glanced up at the sky. "Better get moving," he said. "Looks like there's a shower on the way."

He was right. We had barely finished loading our gear onto a large truck when a brilliant flash of lightning lit the sky. The thunder that followed soon after was almost deafening.

"I thought this was the dry season," Mom said as we quickly scrambled into the truck.

"This is dry," Jim told her.

The sound of the rain drumming on the truck roof was deafening. It was as if we were going through a gigantic car wash. Within minutes the road was transformed into a river of churning brown mud. Jim gunned the engine and ploughed on, even though rain was bucketing against the window. He couldn't possibly see where he was going. I've been on plenty of white-knuckle rides at theme parks, but this one beat them all.

Then someone turned off the tap, and the sky was clear again. Sunlight shone like liquid gold on the flooded roadway and wet, dripping leaves.

Jim chuckled. "You ought to be here during the wet," he said. "It pours like that for days."

M om wanted to go downriver right away, but Jim said it would take a while to prepare the dugout. They were having trouble with the outboard motor. He didn't want it to break down on us.

Mom spent the afternoon helping out in the local

infirmary. There was no hospital in Impfondo, but Mandy was a specially trained nurse. She did what she could to help the sick villagers who came there every day.

"She does wonders," Mom told me afterwards. "But it's pretty basic, I'm afraid. I hate to think how many people must die here every year from easily preventable diseases."

Marcellin showed me around the village while Mom was working. The locals seemed to know all about Dad's disappearance. They were very kind and sympathetic. They apparently didn't think it was the least bit strange for us to have come all this way to look for him.

A few Pygmies were around the area. Marcellin said they often came to trade with the villagers. It was my first chance to see them up close. You really couldn't tell how small they were unless you stood right next to them. Their bodies were well proportioned. I noticed a lot of the men had their teeth filed to points, which looked kind of scary, but they seemed friendly enough.

Flocks of children followed me wherever I went, staring and giggling.

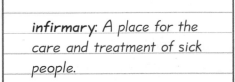

infirmary: A place for the care and treatment of sick people.

I guess I looked weird to them with my pale skin and long hair. Their own hair was cut really short, which made sense in this kind of weather. They had the most gorgeous dark brown eyes I have ever seen. They looked like mini-models. I felt quite plain and clumsy in comparison.

I was amazed how quickly the sun set in this part of the world. There was hardly any twilight at all. By 7:00 that night it was pitch black.

After dinner, Jim showed us some maps of the area. He pointed out the various villages along the Likouala-aux-Herbes River. Dad was last seen leaving a place called Epéna. His empty dugout was found near Edzama. That meant he was most likely somewhere in between. It wasn't a huge distance—about 30 miles—but the thick rain forest and swamps were almost impassable on foot. Jim said Dad would have to zigzag around the swamps. It might explain why he hadn't turned up at any of the villages yet.

Mom and I both decided on an early night. Jim said the dugout was all set to go, so we planned to leave at first light in the morning.

impassable: Impossible to cross or travel over.

Even though I felt dead tired, it was hard to get to sleep. In the hot, sticky darkness, I could hear bats shrieking in the nearby palm trees, along with the calls of other, larger animals.

The voices of the rain forest continued well into the night. But eventually the heat and the noise couldn't keep me awake any longer. I drifted off to sleep.

By sunrise we were already on the river.

It seemed as if the entire village had gathered to see us off. They waved and cheered as the outboard motor spluttered into life and sent our dugout ploughing through the still, muddy water. You would have thought we were lifelong friends rather than a pair of strangers they hadn't met until the day before.

Jim offered to come with us, but Marcellin was worried about the extra weight. The heavier the boat was, the lower it would sit in the water. That meant we were much more likely to run aground or hit a submerged log. We had a two-way radio to keep in touch. A Canadian friend of Jim's, who owned a light plane, offered to scout the river for us from the air. He was due any day now. Jim promised to let us know if he spotted anything.

The first leg of our journey was along a man-made canal that linked Impfondo with the Tanga River. It was a lot narrower than I expected. It was only about three to five feet wide in most places—and clogged with mats of floating weed. Marcellin slowed the dugout to a crawl as we threaded our way from one patch of open water to another. The rain forest canopy closed in above our heads, blocking out the sun. It was like traveling through a tiny green tunnel. Branches and palm fronds hung down close to the water. We kept ducking our heads to avoid them.

One time I felt something land on my shoulder. At first I thought it was a piece of vine or something, but then it started wriggling. I turned my head slowly and saw a small green snake sitting there.

Just as I was about to start screaming, Marcellin casually leaned forward. He flicked the snake into the water.

"Green mamba," he told me as we watched it skim gracefully away. "Very dangerous."

I shivered, suddenly realizing why the antivenin kits were such a necessity.

After that Marcellin had Mom sit in the prow of the boat. She had a long stick so she could beat on the overhanging plant life. Any snakes would hopefully be knocked off before

canopy: Highest layer of tree branches in the rain forest.

we passed under them. Mom didn't seem too thrilled about this, especially when a large python tried to wrap itself around the stick. But she stuck to the job, and we didn't have any more uninvited passengers.

Around mid-morning we met a woman paddling her dugout upriver toward Impfondo. She was taking a load of fresh fish to sell at the market. We decided to buy some from her for lunch. Then we stopped at a wooden platform where the canal joined the Tanga River. Marcellin cooked the fish for us over an open fire. We topped off the meal with a sweet, juicy pineapple we brought with us from Impfondo. It was certainly far more refreshing than the water in our canteens. That water tasted so strongly of chlorine that we might as well have been drinking out of a heated swimming pool.

We made much better time from then on. The Tanga was wider than the canal. There also was far less floating weed to slow us down. Marcellin gunned the outboard, and we scooted along at full throttle through the lush, green rain forest.

By late afternoon we reached the Likouala-aux-Herbes—the River of Grasses as Marcellin called it. It certainly lived up to its name. What I first thought were grassy riverbanks stretching to either side turned out to be islands of floating weed. They drifted slowly with the current, forming little hills and valleys as they moved. I thought we could stop and have a snack on one of them. But Marcellin said they wouldn't support the weight of a small dog, let alone the three of us.

It wasn't far to Epéna. We arrived just before sunset. Apparently we were expected, because a large crowd had gathered to greet us. I thought we'd spend the night in our tents. But a representative of the village insisted that we stay at the government house. This was a large, tin-roofed building where officials from Impfondo and Brazzaville stayed when they came to visit. We thanked him for his hospitality and set up our hammocks in the room provided for us. It was a bit hot inside, but at least we wouldn't have to worry about any leopards. The house was built to keep animals out.

We had barely settled in when there was a knock at the door. It was one of the villagers. He looked really worried. Mom asked Marcellin what was wrong.

"He wants to know if you can help his son," Marcellin told her. "The boy was bitten by a snake yesterday and is very sick."

"Of course," Mom said, quickly grabbing her bag. "Tell him to show me where he is."

We followed the man to one of the many stick-and-mud huts dotted around the government house. A boy about my age was lying on a heap of dried leaves on the floor. His left foot and ankle were swollen to about twice their normal size. I could see two deep puncture marks where the snake's fangs had pierced his skin. A woman I assumed to be his mother was kneeling beside him. She was cradling the boy's head in her hands.

"We need to get that bandage off for a start," Mom said. She pointed to the strip of cloth tied up tightly around the boy's leg. "It's probably doing more harm than good."

I was amazed at how calm she sounded, as if she dealt with problems like this every day. I'm sure she didn't have many snakebite victims turning up at her office back home.

Mom gently untwisted the tourniquet. Judging by the boy's face, this helped reduce the pain a bit, although he still looked bad. "What sort of treatment have they given him so far?" she asked.

Marcellin spoke briefly with the parents, then turned to Mom. "They have tried the traditional cure," he said. "But it does not appear to have done any good."

"And what cure is that, exactly?"

Marcellin looked down at his feet. He seemed deeply embarrassed. "Salt water is placed in the right ear if the bite is on the left foot. It is placed in the left ear for a bite on the right foot. This is foolish, I know."

Mom raised her eyebrows but kept her thoughts about the usefulness of this treatment to herself. "Do they know what sort of snake it was?"

Marcellin again relayed the question to the boy's parents.

"A black one," he said. "Most probably a cobra."

"All right," Mom said. "I'll give him a shot of antivenin and see if that helps."

She fished about in her bag for one of the snakebite

tourniquet: A tight bandage used to stop bleeding or the movement of venom.

kits. The boy's parents held him still while Mom administered a series of injections in and around the bite. The poor boy howled with pain. I hoped his parents understood what was happening. Otherwise they might have thought Mom was killing him.

"Well," Mom said. "All we can do now is wait. I just hope the antivenin is still effective. It really should be kept in a refrigerator."

"What will happen if it doesn't work?" I asked.

"He'll probably die," Mom told me.

We returned to the government hut for dinner, but I didn't feel much like eating. I kept thinking about the boy. I pictured him lying there on his bed of leaves, tears streaming down his face.

Mom and I went to the hut to check on the boy a few hours later. He seemed to be resting more comfortably now. He even managed a small smile when he saw us enter. It looked as if he was going to make it after all.

"You did it, Mom!" I said, throwing my arms around her. "He's going to be okay."

Mom smiled. "Yes," she said. "He is."

She was strangely thoughtful as we made our way to the government house.

"What's the matter?" I asked her.

"Oh, nothing," she said. She looked around at the stick-and-mud huts of the village. Smoke curled lazily above their grass-thatched roofs. The air smelled of palm oil and frying meat. "When I was in medical school, my friends and I often talked about working in a place like this. We thought it would be a chance to practice some real medicine, you know? Not just prescribe pills for people with upset stomachs and runny noses."

"Why didn't you?" I asked.

"I don't know," Mom said. "I met your father and started up a practice. Then you came along . . ." She shrugged. "It just didn't happen, that's all."

"It's not too late," I told her. "You could do it now if you wanted. I love it here."

Mom was silent a moment, then she laughed. "Maybe," she said. "But it wouldn't pay the mortgage. Besides, I can't just throw away everything I've worked for all these years. I run a successful practice. People depend on me. And then there's your education to think about." She shook her head. "No, I'd be crazy to even consider it."

> **mortgage**: Loan taken out, usually from a bank, to buy a house.

"But just think how much good you could do," I said.

"You saved a boy's life today. How often does that happen back home?"

"It simply wouldn't be practical," Mom told me.

"But—"

"But nothing," Mom said sharply. "I think one dreamer in the family is more than enough, don't you?"

From her tone, I knew there was no point arguing any further. I know Mom only wanted what was best for me, but sometimes you have to take a chance. At least, that's what Dad said. "A person's reach should exceed his or her grasp," he used to say—or something like that, anyway.

However, that probably wasn't what Mom wanted to hear just then. For once I kept my mouth shut. We walked the rest of the way to the government house in silence.

As I crawled into my hammock that night, I wondered where my dad could be at that moment. I could hear the rain falling. The forest was very quiet, probably because the animals were staying in their shelters. I hoped Dad had found a dry place to spend the night.

Suddenly, I felt very nervous not knowing where my father was or if he was okay. Mom and I were so close. Yet looking at how dense the rain forest was along the river made me realize that finding him could be almost impossible. But I knew we would not give up until we did.

The rain finally stopped, and the animals started calling to one another. Listening to the sounds of the creatures in the forest made me feel better than the pattering of the rain. I finally went to sleep.

Chapter 5
Green Darkness

THE MORNING started off well enough. We gave Jim a call before we left Epéna. Although there was still no word about Dad, he told us his pilot friend had just arrived. He would start scouting the river that afternoon. So things were looking pretty good. It seemed only a matter of time before we tracked down Dad one way or another.

Mom's patient was doing well. We visited him before we left and found the boy sitting up in bed with a huge smile on his face. His parents solemnly presented Mom with a basket of fresh fruit. Mom said it was the most rewarding payment she ever received.

We'd been traveling for a few hours when it happened. Despite the mats of grass clogging the sides of the river, there was a clear channel along the middle, and we were making good time. I can picture the spot exactly, even though I'd probably never be able to find it again.

We rounded a sharp bend, coming close to the right-hand bank. The wall of the rain forest rose before us, woven through with ferns and ropes of flowering vines. Clouds of butterflies whirled about our heads. Their wings glistened in the sunlight as if splattered with bright paint.

Suddenly we heard a loud PLOP! A huge wave appeared from nowhere. It swamped the dugout and tossed all three of us into the river. I remember thrashing about wildly as the water closed above my head. Somehow I managed to reach one of the mats of floating grass and haul myself up onto it. The next thing I knew, I was lying on my back, gasping for air. The rain forest canopy slid slowly by on either side.

"Mom!" I shouted. "Marcellin! Can you hear me?" There was no reply.

I don't know how long I was unconscious. It could have been hours.

The floating island had snagged on the riverbank while I was still out. My first thought was to get ashore as quickly as I could. I remembered the crocodiles I saw earlier from the dugout. They were cruising along the river like submerged logs. Only their cold, luminous eyes were visible above the waterline. I didn't want to end up providing a tasty lunch for one of them.

It was impossible to walk on the mat of weed. My feet just went straight through it. I ended up wriggling on my belly. Even then there were times when I thought the grass was going to give way beneath my weight. I was sure it would send me plunging face-first into the river below.

Eventually I made it. Panting and sweating, I crawled up onto the bank and collapsed in a heap. I knew there was no point calling for help. There was no telling how far I'd drifted while I was unconscious, but it must have been quite a distance. Otherwise, Mom and Marcellin would have found me by now. Unless, of course, something had happened to them. I felt a sudden stab of panic. What if they'd drowned? I told myself not to be ridiculous. Marcellin knew what he was doing. He wouldn't let anything happen to Mom. They were probably looking for me right now where the dugout capsized, not

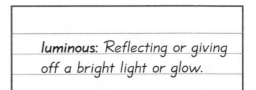

luminous: *Reflecting or giving off a bright light or glow.*

realizing that I'd drifted so far downstream.

There wasn't any point waiting around for them to find me. Climbing to my feet, I decided to head back toward Epéna. That way I was bound to run into them sooner or later.

As I started off, I wondered where the wave that engulfed us had come from. The river was perfectly flat again now, like a mud-streaked mirror. Perhaps the wave came from a large motorboat, but surely we would have heard it coming. There was nothing but that strange plopping sound, like a huge stone hitting the water. Was it an animal then? Marcellin said there were no hippos in this part of the river. But what else could make a splash that size?

I suddenly stopped dead in my tracks. The answer was obvious. I couldn't believe I hadn't thought of it before. It wasn't a hippo that made the wave but something at least twice as big. Something that had lived in these rivers for more than 65 million years. Mokele-Mbembe!

It was the only explanation. Dad was right after all. It did exist. And we had come within less than 20 feet of one. If I hadn't been so busy trying not to drown, I might have seen it with my own eyes!

> **engulfed**: *Flowed over and enclosed.*

Wait until Dad heard about this. Perhaps he'd even let me help track down the dinosaur. All we needed was one decent photo, and then we could prove it to the world.

First, of course, I had to find Mom and Marcellin. Taking a deep breath, I trudged on through the rain forest. How hard could it be? I just needed to follow the river back upstream. Surely it couldn't take me more than a couple of hours at the most. I began moving through the forest.

The going was a lot harder than I expected. You couldn't tell where the riverbank ended and the floating grass began. Time after time, I put my foot down on what I thought was solid ground, and then find myself suddenly waist-deep in water. The trees were so tightly jammed together in places that I couldn't squeeze through no matter how hard I tried. Curtains of ropy vines dangled from every branch. I was forever tripping over roots and unseen potholes.

The only alternative was to wade along the water's edge where I'd be easy prey for any passing crocodiles. The thought of snakes dropping down as I passed made my skin crawl. But at least I didn't have to worry about them biting me in half.

Fortunately, the rain forest was crisscrossed with animal trails. This made progress a little easier in places. Judging by the piles of fresh dung I came across, some pretty large beasts passed that way—buffalo, perhaps, or even elephants. But I didn't run into any. They probably heard me approaching for ages and decided to make themselves scarce. That suited me just fine. The less I saw the local wildlife, the better.

It took me a surprisingly long time to realize I was lost. I thought the trail I was following ran parallel to the river, although it was impossible to know for sure. Hardly any light penetrated the rain forest canopy. The close-packed trees walled me in on either side. When I finally decided to stop and check, the water had simply disappeared.

I hunted around for a while but got nowhere. I was probably just going around in circles for all I knew. It seemed pointless to keep going. According to the map Jim had shown us, the rain forest stretched in a huge unbroken mass in every direction. I could spend years wandering through it and never find my way out.

It was getting darker now, the emerald twilight deepening to pitch black. I remembered Marcellin saying that snakes and other animals were less likely to cross open ground. I stopped at the first small clearing I came to and prepared to settle down for the night. My legs felt like sacks of jelly. I stretched out

68

on a bed of stiff, prickly grass.

Mosquitoes swarmed around me, but they were the least of my worries. Marcellin had told me about poisonous millipedes and swarms of driver ants that could strip the flesh from your bones. I just hoped that none of them would come my way.

I huddled inside my clothes, trying to expose as little bare skin as I could. I could hear animals slinking through the leafy darkness around me. Occasionally a loud cry rang out. I held my breath, praying that its owner was headed in a different direction.

I was hot, thirsty, aching in every joint—and frightened almost out of my wits. But eventually sheer exhaustion overwhelmed my fears and discomfort, and I sank into a deep, dreamless sleep.

At the time, I couldn't care less if I never woke up again.

I did, of course. Enough light filtered down through the rain forest canopy

for me to tell that the sun had risen. But I had no idea of the exact time. It could just as easily have been early morning or late afternoon.

The first thing I noticed was that nothing appeared to have eaten me during the night. The second was that I wasn't alone.

I scrambled to my feet, choking back a scream.

The Pygmy, who was watching me silently, cocked his head to one side. Unlike those I saw in Impfondo, he was wearing nothing but a loincloth around his hips. He carried what looked like a homemade crossbow. A case full of arrows was slung over his shoulder.

Once I recovered from my initial shock, I realized a young boy was peering at me around the man's body. You couldn't really blame him, I guess. I was probably the last thing anyone expected to find way out here in the rain forest.

I felt a bit silly about how I reacted.

The two were obviously just out hunting.

"Mbote," I said, bowing slightly. That was what Marcellin said whenever he met someone in the village. I assumed it meant hello.

The Pygmy grinned, flashing his filed teeth, and proceeded to rattle off several sentences in reply. Mbote seemed to be in there somewhere, but none of the other words sounded even vaguely familiar.

I shook my head apologetically. "Sorry," I said. "I don't understand."

It was his turn to look confused. I doubt he had ever heard English before. The locals in Impfondo and Epéna certainly didn't speak it. I might have had more luck with French, but the only two words I knew were "eau-de-cologne" and "crouton." That just left charades. I can't say I'm particularly good at them, but it seemed worth a shot.

I slowly pointed to both the hunter and his son, trying to look happy and contented. Then I pointed to myself with a look of bewilderment. Then I shaded my eyes with one hand and looked from side to side. Translation: "I'm searching for my father." It was hard

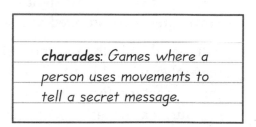

charades: Games where a person uses movements to tell a secret message.

to know whether I got the message across or not. Then I had an idea. "Epéna?" I asked, pointing in various directions. "Epéna?"

That seemed to do the trick. Both the boy and his father nodded vigorously. They motioned for me to follow them. Then they turned and headed off in exactly the opposite direction to the one I would have chosen. (Which just showed how little hope there was of me finding my own way out of the rain forest.) Feeling extremely relieved, I hurried after them.

They set a quick pace. Even the boy, who was half my size, easily outpaced me. They slipped through gaps in the trees where none seemed to exist and never once lost their footing. It was a struggle keeping up with them right from the start. Within 15 minutes, I was soaked in sweat and panting for breath. No matter how hard I pushed myself, however, I just kept getting further and further behind.

Once or twice, I lost sight of them altogether. Fortunately they stopped and waited for me.

It was dreadfully hot under the trees. I couldn't remember when I last had anything to drink, and my throat was dry. Just when I thought I couldn't go a step further, the father stopped. He pointed to some thick vines snaking through the branches around us. As the boy and I watched, he took an arrow from his case. He used its sharpened end to cut several of the vines. Then he handed each of us a piece.

I had no idea what to do with it, but the boy obviously did. Tilting his head back, he held one cut end of the vine above his mouth and let the clear, watery sap dribble into it. His father nodded, gesturing for me to do the same.

I was thirsty enough to try anything. The sap was cool and almost tasteless. It certainly was a huge improvement to the chlorinated water I was drinking before. The boy's father must have noticed how greedily I gulped it down. He immediately handed me another piece of vine, which I drained eagerly. I felt better after that and managed not to fall so far behind when we set off again.

I was amazed that the boy and his father seemed so much at home in the rain forest. They strolled through it as if cruising the aisles of a huge supermarket. The water vines were their drink machines. The incredible assortment of tropical plants offered a far wider, and tastier, range of

> **assortment**: *A variety or collection of different things or items.*

food than any fast-food restaurant. Whenever my strength started to go down, the father cut some pods from one of the trees. He gave me the sweet-tasting beans inside. Not only did this perk me up, but most of my aches and pains disappeared as well.

I began to feel more confident about Dad's chances of surviving in the rain forest. As long as he had the guides to look after him, he'd be all right.

Knowing that put an even bigger spring in my step. It's funny how much difference a little optimism makes. Before the rain forest seemed like a crazy maze, brimming with unseen terrors. Now I just marveled at the sheer beauty and wonder of the place. People who had trouble believing that dinosaurs still roamed this hidden paradise were those who'd never been here.

Personally, I had no doubts at all. You only had to look around to realize it was quite possible for creatures like Mokele-Mbembe to exist in a place like this. In fact, I would have been amazed if they didn't. I just needed to find Dad, and then we could prove it once and for all.

Chapter 6

The Last Dinosaur

Fact: Although most reports of undiscovered animals turn out to be cases of mistaken identity, cryptozoologists believe they are still worth investigating.

UNTIL NOW the boy and his father had acted like they didn't have a care in the world. Whenever a snake crossed our path, the father pushed it away as casually as we might brush away a fly. Every other animal we saw was fair game. He already had caught a pair of small monkeys and just missed an antelope.

For some reason, however, they now were extremely wary. I found myself tiptoeing behind them, as if walking on broken glass.

We followed the river for some time, presumably heading back toward Epéna. But this section of it looked unfamiliar. It was a lot narrower than I remembered, and the far bank was quite steep. Here and there I could see patches of shadow that might have been the mouths of large, half-submerged caves.

The plants were different as well. One type of vine I never saw before was particularly common. They were strung through the treetops like giant holiday decorations, dripping with beautiful white flowers. They also had clusters of yellowish green fruit about the size of oranges. What struck me the most about them was that they were apparently one of the few plants that the Pygmies didn't eat. In fact, both the boy and his father stayed away from them. They often went out of their way to circle those places where the vines were thickest. This seemed rather strange to me. After all, even if the plants were poisonous or something, they were hardly likely to attack us as we went by.

We were halfway through one of these detours when I heard it. Imagine being outside a packed football game when the winning goal is scored. That's what it sounded like. It was an ear-splitting roar that made even the loudest leopard's cry seem nothing more than a whisper in comparison.

I felt the hair stand up on the back of my neck. Surely only one animal in the world could make a noise like that!

This was the moment I'd been waiting for. I immediately started toward the river. I'd only managed a few steps before the father grabbed my arm. He dragged me deeper into the forest. Just for a moment I thought I glimpsed a huge, reddish brown shape rearing up out of the water. Then the rain forest closed around me, and I lost sight of it completely.

Both the boy and his father were obviously terrified. They stared at me in amazement. It was the way you might look at someone who had just tried to throw themselves in front of a truck.

"Mokele-Mbembe?" I asked breathlessly.

The father's grip on my arm tightened, as if the mere name filled him with dread. I was desperate for a closer look but didn't want to offend him by trying to pull free. I probably couldn't have anyway—his grip was like iron.

Suddenly there was a loud splash—just like I'd heard moments before the wave swamped our dugout. The great beast had obviously returned to the water. And in a hurry, too, by the sound of it.

At first I had no idea what scared it off. Surely no rain forest predators were large enough to prey on it. (I certainly hoped not. Anything that big could eat us for breakfast.) I noticed, however, that both the boy and his

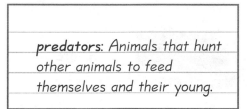

predators: Animals that hunt other animals to feed themselves and their young.

father were peering upwards. But there was nothing to see through the thick palm fronds. I got the impression they were listening to something up in the air.

Then I heard it as well.

It took me a few moments to recognize the sound. For a while I actually thought a swarm of enormous bees might descend upon us. As the low-pitched drone got louder, I finally realized what it was. I bolted toward the river.

The boy and his father followed close behind, but they didn't try to stop me this time. Maybe they could tell by the look on my face that it wouldn't do them any good.

As I burst through the wall of trees lining the riverbank, I saw a small single-engine plane circling overhead. It was the most beautiful sight in the world.

I screamed and waved for all I was worth. For one dreadful moment, I thought the pilot didn't see me. Then he waggled the plane's wings in acknowledgment, and I knew everything was going to be all right.

I half expected the Pygmies to be startled by the plane's appearance, but they seemed to take it in their stride. They must have more contact with the modern world than I realized. It suddenly occurred to me that Mokele-Mbembe must be quite a fearsome creature for them to be so afraid of it.

The plane did one last circuit, then headed back upriver. As I watched it slowly disappear from sight, I knew my troubles would soon be over. All I had to do was wait for a boat to come along and pick me up. I sat down on the riverbank and did just that.

Mom didn't wait for Marcellin to run their dugout ashore. As soon as they were close to the riverbank, she vaulted over the side and splashed toward me. Luckily, no crocodiles were around. I hate to think what she would have done to them if they got in her way.

Next thing I knew, her arms were so tightly wrapped around me I thought I'd burst.

circuit: *A circular path or route around a certain area or territory.*

"Oh, Gina!" she said. "I'm so happy we found you! Are you all right?"

"I'm fine, Mom," I told her. "The Pygmies looked after me."

I felt Mom's bear hug slacken a bit. She glanced around the riverbank, then looked down at me, frowning slightly. "What Pygmies?" she said.

I laughed, turning my head toward where the boy and his father had been sitting patiently for several hours now. Only they weren't there anymore.

I stared stupidly at the remains of the fire. The father had roasted one of the monkeys for our supper. The ground was littered with fruit, but the Pygmies themselves appeared to have melted silently back into the rain forest.

"They were here a moment ago," I told Mom. "A father and his little boy. We were on our way to Epéna when I heard the plane. They stayed with me all this time to make sure I was safe." It couldn't have been easy for them either. I remembered how the father kept scanning the river. It was as if he feared Mokele-Mbembe might rise up out of the water at any minute. But he refused to budge until he knew for certain that I would be all right.

"We must find them, Mom," I said. "After all, they saved my life. I want to at least say thank you."

Marcellin had joined us by now. He put a hand on my shoulder. "I am afraid there would be no point, mademoiselle," he said. "The forest folk cannot be found unless they choose to be. Besides, I do not think they would want you to thank them. They are a noble people. To them, it would be unthinkable not to help you—just as they would help anyone in need. It is their way."

I guess he was right. But I still felt bad. Even though I was a complete stranger—and a foreigner as well—the Pygmies had treated me like one of their own. They even braved Mokele-Mbembe himself to see that I didn't come to any harm. Friends don't come much better than that.

"I suppose we should get going," Mom said. "It'll be dark soon."

"Any word about Dad?" I asked her as we headed for the dugout.

She stopped in midstep, slapping a hand to her forehead. "That's right!" she said. "I was meaning to tell you right away, but I forgot."

noble: High standards and morals.

My heart lurched inside me. "Tell me what?"

"We found him," Mom said. "Apparently he was—"

She didn't get any further. I spun around, grabbing her shoulders in both hands. "Where? How? When?" I babbled. "What happened to him? Is he all right?"

I saw Mom and Marcellin exchange glances. Something about the way they looked at each other made my blood run cold. "What's wrong?" I said. "He's okay, isn't he? I mean, he's not . . ."

I couldn't bring myself to say the word.

"No, no," Mom said hastily. "Of course not. It's just that he was in an accident, that's all. Nothing life threatening, but . . ." She ran her fingers through her hair. She looked exhausted. It occurred to me just how tough the past 24 hours or so must have been on her. "His right leg was in pretty bad shape," she told me. "Apparently he cut it when his dugout overturned, and infection is always a problem in this kind of climate. I'm afraid I had to amputate."

"You mean cut it off?"

Mom nodded.

I guess it wasn't the end of the world. After all, plenty of people managed to achieve remarkable things with worse disabilities than that. But it was a bit of a shock. Dad was always so active. He loved hiking. Still, knowing him, he wouldn't let something like this cramp his style. Not for long, anyway.

"He will be all right though, won't he?" I said. "I mean, it's not like he's going to die or anything?"

"His condition was quite serious," Mom said in her best doctor's voice. "But he's not in any immediate danger now."

"Where is he?" I asked. "Can I see him?"

"Of course you can. I'm keeping him in Epéna until he's strong enough to fly back to Brazzaville."

I wanted to ask more questions, but Mom said she could answer them on the way. After all, the sooner we got moving, the quicker we'd be in Epéna. That made sense to me.

As we clambered into the dugout, I noticed Marcellin looking at something.

"What is it?" I asked him.

He pointed at a large, circular depression in the riverbank. It was the size of a dinner plate, with three rounded points at one end.

Marcellin shook his head. "It looks like a footprint," he said.

"But I don't know of any animal that leaves tracks like this one. I've never seen anything like it."

I grinned. "Pretty impressive for a wild goose, eh?" I said.

"Goose?" Marcellin looked at me strangely. He must have thought I was out of my mind. "What do you mean?"

"Doesn't matter," I told him. "I was just thinking out loud."

I really wanted Dad to be there when I broke the news about Mokele-Mbembe. Even on one leg, he'd be jumping through the roof when I told him.

I could hardly wait.

"Remember," Mom said as we entered the government house. "He's been through quite an ordeal. Don't be surprised if some of the things he says don't make much sense."

I nodded. Mom explained everything on the way back to Epéna. Obviously I wasn't the only Patrioni who owed their life to the kindness and courage of the Pygmies. Dad's boat collided with something midstream and snapped completely in half. Although the guides and he managed to get ashore all right,

Dad's leg was badly injured in the accident. He couldn't walk. Rather than just leaving him there, the Pygmies insisted on carrying him out of the rain forest with them. It must have been a painfully slow process, which explained why we hadn't heard from him. Jim's pilot friend finally spotted the group in a clearing not far from Epéna. A rescue party was organized to pick them up.

Dad was lying on a makeshift bed set up in the same room we used during our previous visit. His face was flushed. The flickering gaslight carved deep hollows in his cheeks. Although Mom warned me what to expect, I was shocked at how frail he looked. He certainly wasn't going to be jumping anywhere for a while, let alone through the roof. Fighting back tears, I hovered in the doorway for a moment.

"Dad?" I said softly. "It's me. Gina."

Dad didn't have enough strength to lift his head from the pillow. His smile, however, was as wide and warm as ever as he slowly turned toward me. "About time," he said. "I think your mother's been taking this no visitors routine a bit too far, don't you?" He pulled a face. "Doctors, eh? Think they know everything, don't they?"

Mom hadn't told him about me being missing. It would have been too upsetting for him. Right now all that mattered was him getting better.

"Yeah," I said. "Give them a stethoscope and they think they own the place. How are you feeling?"

"Surprisingly good, actually. I think it's all those painkillers your mom's been feeding me." Dad looked at me a moment, then laughed. "You don't have to stand way over there, you know," he said. "I'm not contagious or anything."

All of the tears I'd been holding back suddenly brimmed over and streamed down my face. "Oh, Dad," I said as I rushed to the bed and threw my arms around him. "I was so scared! I thought something terrible had happened to you."

"Hey, hey," Dad said, gently stroking my hair. "I'm still in one piece. Well, most of me, anyway. I guess Mom told you about the leg, huh?"

I nodded bravely but could not keep the look of sadness from my face.

"Ah, well, not to worry." Dad slapped his remaining leg with one hand. "I'll finally be able to use all those odd socks I collected over the years."

It wasn't much of a joke, but I laughed anyway.

"That's better," Dad said. He glanced over my shoulder a moment, then leaned in closer, almost whispering in my ear. "Where's your mom?"

"I think she's fixing me something to eat," I told him. "Why? Would you like me to get her?"

Dad shook his head. "No, no, no. Don't do that. I just have to be a bit careful. She thinks I'm delirious, you see."

"Delirious?" I said. I couldn't figure out what he was talking about.

"Yeah. You know—a bit crazy and everything," he said with a sparkle in his eye.

"Why would she think that?"

Dad suddenly grabbed hold of my wrist. "Because I saw him, Gina! With my own two eyes! I saw him!"

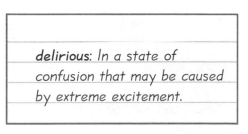

delirious: In a state of confusion that may be caused by extreme excitement.

"Who?" I said, half thinking that Mom may have been right after all. Dad didn't seem to be making much sense. Perhaps the painkillers had gone to his head.

"Why, Mokele-Mbembe, of course!" Dad said. There was a feverish gleam in his eyes, and something else as well. Triumph, perhaps. "He surfaced right in front of us. Snapped the dugout in half like a toothpick with one blow of his neck. Must have thought we were invading his territory or something."

I was dying to tell Dad about my own close encounters with the dinosaur. But then he'd know I'd been lost in the rain forest. Now, I didn't need to. In fact, it was better this way. He could have his moment of glory all to himself.

"That's fantastic, Dad," I said. "Wait till people hear

about this. You'll be famous. Everyone will know about your discovery."

"No, I won't," he said wearily. "Nobody will believe me. And why should they? I didn't get any evidence to prove what happened. No photographs. Nothing. I'll be like those weirdos who claim they were kidnapped by Big Foot or abducted by aliens. Just someone for the newspapers to make fun of."

He had a point, of course. "What about your guides?" I said. "They must have seen it too."

"Sure they did. But they won't admit it. They say anyone who sees Mokele-Mbembe and tells people about it will die." Dad shook his head. "It's hard to fight such a strong superstition. No wonder it's so hard to gather eyewitness reports."

Dad was right. What he needed was hard, scientific proof. Even the footprint Marcellin and I had found probably wasn't enough. "You can always try again," I said. "Once you're feeling better, of course. After all, we know Mokele-Mbembe is out there now. It's simply a matter of finding him. Then we can get that photo we need, and people will have to believe us."

> **superstition:** *A belief resulting from fear of the unknown.*

Dad looked at me. "Us?"

"Sure," I said. "I couldn't let you come back here on your own, now could I? Not after the mess you made this time around."

"Oh, yes?" Dad asked. "And what about your mother? I think she might have something to say about that, don't you?"

I thought about what she told me after she saved that young boy's life. Who knows, maybe she'd even want to come with us.

"You might be surprised," I said. "She has dreams of her own. Everyone does. Some are just a bit crazier than others, that's all."

"You mean like mine?" Dad asked with a crooked smile on his face.

"Exactly," I told him. "But that doesn't mean they can't come true. You've proved that already—no matter what anyone else thinks."

Dad took my hand. He looked tired and happy, and rather proud, all at the same time. I probably did too. It was certainly how I felt.

"I guess I have at that," he said. "Not bad for a fruitcake, eh?"

I blushed, remembering what I'd written in my project book just a few weeks before. It was amazing how much had changed since then.

Next time Career Week rolled around, I'd be the first one up there. Brad Jenkins could laugh himself sick for all I cared. I would not feel embarrassed by what my dad did for a living.

I already knew what I was going to say:

"My father is Raphael Patrioni. He dreamed of finding the world's last living dinosaur—and he did!"

Rain Forest Facts

Rain forests are home to about half of all the earth's animal species. Around 140 of these species are driven into extinction every day as forests are cleared to make room for farmland.

Mokele-Mbembe is said to be 16 to 32 feet long with a snakelike head and a long, powerful tail. The only known animals that fit this description are the sauropod dinosaurs, such as the Diplodocus. Mokele-Mbembe means "The Stopper of Rivers" in the native language.

Some people fear that animals such as chimpanzees and mountain gorillas may be hunted to extinction. They are used to provide meat for diners in expensive restaurants.

About one million people are bitten by snakes every year. Between 30,000 and 40,000 of them die, mainly because they don't receive proper medical treatment.

Crocodiles first appeared on Earth around the same time as dinosaurs. They have survived relatively unchanged for over one hundred million years.

Many of the medicines we use today come from rain forest plants. Aspirin, a painkiller, is one of them. Other medicines from plants are used to treat heart disease and arthritis.

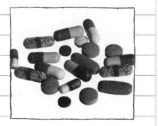

93

Monkeys are one of the Pygmies' favorite foods, but most of their diet is made up of fruits and vegetables. They gather these from the wild plants found in the rain forest.

It is estimated that more than 50 million species of insects, beetles, and spiders inhabit the world's rain forests. Once, a scientist found 50 different kinds of ants living on a single tree. Most new species found in the wild today are insects.

Dinosaurs are sometimes named after people or after the place where they are found. The Lambeosaurus was named in honor of Canadian fossil hunter, Lawrence Lamb.

Where to from Here?

You've just read the story of Gina's survival in search of the last living dinosaur. Here are some ideas for finding more stories about survival and mysterious creatures.

The Library

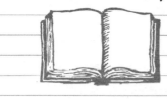

Some books you might enjoy include:
- *Loch* by Paul Zindel
- *The Sign of the Beaver* by Elizabeth George Speare
- *Downriver* by Will Hobbs
- *Hostage* by Edward Myers

Here is a nonfiction book to try:
Field Guide to the Sasquatch by Society of Cryptozoology, David George Gordon

TV, Film, and Video

Check TV listings and your local video store and library for films about mysterious and extinct creatures. Some suggestions are:
- *Ancient Mysteries: Bigfoot*
- *In Search of the Loch Ness Monster*

The Internet

Search the Internet, using keywords such as *Mokele-Mbembe, dinosaurs, fossils,* and *cryptozoology*. Also check *http://ucmpl.berkeley.edu/exhibittext/entrance*.

People and Places

If there is a natural history museum nearby, visit it to learn more about dinosaurs and about the earth's rain forests.

The Ultimate Nonfiction Book

Be sure to check out *Fantastic Creatures*, the companion volume to *The Last Dinosaur*. *Fantastic Creatures* describes some of the amazing real and mythical animals that have fascinated people for centuries.

Decide for yourself
where fiction stops
and fact begins.